T5-BYS-367

A Robbie Reader

The Lost Continent of Atlantis

Russell Roberts

Mitchell Lane PUBLISHERS

P.O. Box 196
Hockessin, Delaware 19707
Visit us on the web: www.mitchelllane.com
Comments? email us:
mitchelllane@mitchelllane.com

Where is **?** Atlantis

0 0022 0309063 0

HA CASS COUNTY PUBLIC LIBRARY
400 E. MECHANIC
HARRISONVILLE, MO 64701

Mitchell Lane
PUBLISHERS

Copyright © 2007 by Mitchell Lane Publishers. All rights reserved. No part of this book may be reproduced without written permission from the publisher. Printed and bound in the United States of America.

Printing   1   2   3   4   5   6   7   8   9

A Robbie Reader/Natural Disasters

The Ancient Mystery of Easter Island
The Bermuda Triangle, 1945
Bubonic Plague
Earthquake in Loma Prieta, California, 1989
The Fury of Hurricane Andrew, 1992
Hurricane Katrina, 2005
The Lost Continent of Atlantis
Mt. Vesuvius and the Destruction of Pompeii, A.D. 79
Mudslide in La Conchita, California, 2005
Tsunami Disaster in Indonesia, 2004
Where Did All the Dinosaurs Go?

Library of Congress Cataloging-in-Publication Data
Roberts, Russell, 1953–
    The lost continent of Atlantis / by Russell Roberts.
        p. cm. — (A Robbie reader. Natural disasters)
    Includes bibliographical references and index.
    ISBN 1-58415-496-9 (lib. bdg. : alk. paper)
    1. Atlantis—Juvenile literature. I. Title. II. Series.
GN751.R47 2005
001.94—dc22
                                                                            2005028496

ISBN-10: 1-58415-496-9   ISBN 13: 978-1-58415-496-9

ABOUT THE AUTHOR: Russell Roberts has written and published over 35 books for adults and children on a variety of subjects, including baseball, memory power, business, New Jersey history, and travel. He has also written numerous books for Mitchell Lane, such as *Pedro Menendez de Aviles*, *Philo Farnsworth Invents TV*, *Robert Goddard*, *Bernardo de Galvez*, and *Mt. Vesuvius and the Destruction of Pompeii, A.D. 79*. He lives in Bordentown, New Jersey, with his family and a fat, fuzzy, and crafty calico cat named Rusti.

PHOTO CREDITS: Cover—David Hardy/Photo Researchers; p. 4—Hulton Archive/Getty Images; p. 6—Fox Photos/Getty Images; p. 8—Time Life Pictures/Getty Images; p. 11—Hulton Archive; pp. 12, 20—Barbara Marvis; pp. 14, 18—Sharon Beck; p. 15—Photo Researchers; pp. 17, 22, 24—Jamie Kondrchek.

PUBLISHER'S NOTE: The following story has been thoroughly researched and to the best of our knowledge presents the theories surrounding the real or mythical Atlantis. While every possible effort has been made to ensure accuracy, the publisher will not assume liability for damages caused by inaccuracies in the data and makes no warranty on the accuracy of the information contained herein.

To reflect current usage, we have chosen to use the secular era designations BCE ("before the common era") and CE ("of the common era") instead of the traditional designations BC ("before Christ") and AD (*anno Domini*, "in the year of the Lord").

TABLE OF CONTENTS

Words in **bold** type can be found in the glossary.

Poseidon was the Greek god of the sea. The name Atlantis comes from Atlas, who was one of Poseidon's sons.

CHAPTER ONE

Island Kingdom

Once there was an island kingdom named Atlantis. The name comes from Atlas. He was a Greek god who carried the world on his shoulders. According to Greek **mythology**, Atlas was the eldest son of Poseidon (poe-SIE-dun). Poseidon was the god of the sea.

Atlantis was a large island. It was also a beautiful **paradise**. The ground was rich and **fertile**. Vegetables grew fat and large. Fruit filled the trees. Healing roots and herbs grew everywhere. Animals such as bulls, horses, and elephants roamed the forests.

Atlantis had mountains and waterfalls. Hot and cold water bubbled up from springs. On a

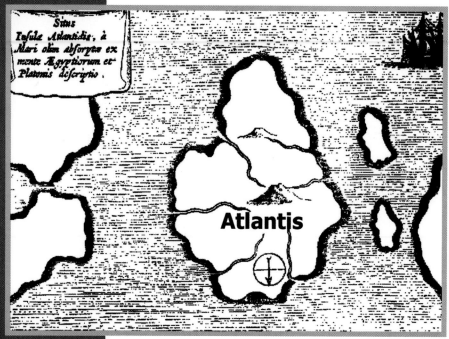

This map, with South at the top, is one artist's idea of what Atlantis looked like and where it was located. It shows a large piece of land in the Atlantic Ocean.

high hill at the center of the island, Poseidon built a home for his wife, Cleito (KLY-toe). He surrounded the home with rings of water and land for his wife's protection.

The people of Atlantis farmed and made things. They traded with other countries. Ships from these other lands filled the harbor in Atlantis. At night a big lighthouse lit their way.

Atlantis ruled a large empire. It was bigger than the size of modern-day Libya (a country in Africa) and Asia combined. It included parts of Europe and North and South America. Atlantis was a good kingdom. Its people were kind, gentle, and caring. They lived in peace. They were **virtuous**.

As the years passed, Atlantis changed. The people argued. They stole and lied. Their armies attacked other countries. Their virtue left them. What was once good became evil.

One day an **earthquake** caused a giant wave. The wave smashed into Atlantis. More earthquakes caused the ground to split open. Atlantis sank into the sea. In one day and night, Atlantis vanished.

This is the sad yet amazing story of Atlantis. There is just one problem with it . . .

We do not know if it is true.

Plato was a very wise and smart man. It is because of Plato that we know about Atlantis. He talked about it in a story. Many people doubt that the story was true.

Plato and Atlantis

Atlantis. Is its story fact or fiction? While people no longer believe in the Greek god Poseidon or his son Atlas, no one is sure about the rest of the story.

One reason we do not know is time. If it existed, Atlantis would have been thriving around eleven thousand years ago. Back then, there were no cameras. There was no television or newspapers. There are no pictures of Atlantis, except for those drawn from people's imaginations.

There is just one account of Atlantis. It is by Plato, a wise and famous Greek philosopher. He lived long ago too. Because he was so wise, people study his writings. Around 350 BCE, he wrote about Atlantis. Plato said the story was true, so people believe it.

But is it? Remember that Plato was a philosopher. He taught lessons with his stories. Maybe Atlantis was simply a lesson. When Atlantis was good, the city was fine. When it turned bad, it was destroyed. Maybe that is the lesson Plato was trying to teach. Maybe he made up the story of Atlantis to teach a lesson about good and evil.

But maybe Plato did not need to make it up. Maybe it really existed. It would still teach the lesson.

Let us say the story of Atlantis is true. If so, how did Plato learn about it?

Long ago people told each other stories. They did so to remember things. The stories were told over and over.

There was a man named Solon who lived many years before Plato. He was also Greek. Solon went to Egypt, where the Egyptians told him about Atlantis. We don't know how the Egyptians knew about Atlantis. It is another little piece of the whole mystery.

Solon brought the story of Atlantis back to Greece from Egypt. However, some people say that when he repeated the story, he made errors. These errors have helped to deepen the mystery of Atlantis.

Solon came back to Greece and told the story of Atlantis. It was repeated for years. Then Plato heard it and wrote it down.

Solon did not speak Egyptian, so he did not understand some of the words the Egyptians spoke. Some people believe that when he tried to change these words into Greek words, he made mistakes. They say some of his words were wrong, and these wrong words got into the story of Atlantis. Did they? We do not know. In the end, Solon's account only adds to the mystery.

A monument to the Pillars of Hercules stands near the Strait of Gilbraltar. According to Plato, Atlantis was located to the west of the Pillars of Hercules.

CHAPTER THREE

Lost Continent

Many things are easily lost. A pen, a book, money . . . One minute they are here, and then they are gone.

But Atlantis was an island that was as big as a **continent**. People call it the Lost Continent. No one knows where it is. How can you lose a continent?

Plato said Atlantis was west of the Pillars of Hercules. This was the old name for two rocks on the eastern side of the Strait of Gibraltar. The strait separates the Atlantic Ocean from the Mediterranean Sea. By saying Atlantis was west of the pillars, Plato meant that it was in the Atlantic.

There is a chain of islands in the Atlantic called the Azores. These islands are the tops of

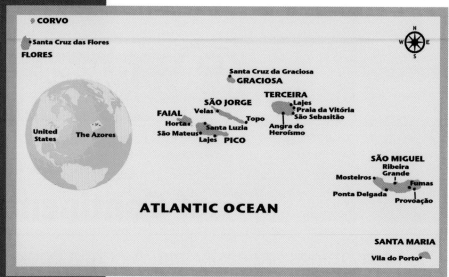

The chain of islands called the Azores is located in the Atlantic Ocean. Some people believe that the Azores reveal the location of Atlantis. They say that the Azores are the tops of mountains reaching up from Atlantis.

mountains poking up out of the sea. Some people say that the mountaintops are from Atlantis.

Some scientists even believe that Atlantis was east, rather than west, of the Strait of Gibraltar. A history professor named K. T. Frost first came up with this theory in 1909. Now many others believe it. If he is right, then Atlantis is in the opposite direction from where many people have been looking.

In 1968, a straight line of stone blocks was discovered at the bottom of the Atlantic

The Strait of Gibraltar as seen from high in the air. The Strait of Gibraltar connects the Mediterranean Sea (top) with the Atlantic Ocean. At some points the strait is only eight miles wide.

Ocean. They are near the islands of Bimini, which are close to Florida. The blocks seem like they used to be above ground. People call the line of blocks the Bimini Road.

Why are these blocks there? Are they part of Atlantis? Some people think so. They say the blocks prove that Atlantis was in the Atlantic Ocean. But others are not so sure. There are broken stone columns in the area. Some people say that the columns are actually made of cement. According to them, barrels of cement fell off a modern-day ship. The barrels rotted away, and the cement mixed with the water to form the columns. If that did indeed happen, did something similar happen to form Bimini Road?

The Atlantic Ocean is still a popular guess about the location of Atlantis. Many people have searched the Atlantic Ocean for the lost island, but they have not found it. Does that mean it never existed? Or does that just mean that people with a different theory, like Professor Frost, are correct?

One very different theory is that Atlantis is in the East China Sea. In the sea, off the southwest coast of Japan, is an island called Yonaguni.

In 1995, a man discovered stone ruins under the water off Yonaguni. Scientists studied them. They believe they are from 8000 BCE. The ruins look to be human-made. They look like other ancient structures in other countries.

What are these ruins? It is another mystery. Once these ruins must have been above ground. Now they are sunk. Are these

Bimini Road is a collection of huge stone blocks arranged in a long straight line. It lies 10 to 15 feet under water. Nobody knows how it got there.

the ruins of Atlantis? Did some people from Atlantis escape the sinking city? Did they travel to other countries? Is that why these ruins resemble others?

Do you see why Atlantis is "lost"? There are many clues about its location, but there are no answers. People look but they do not find it. They are looking right now.

The whole island is not the only thing that is lost. The people of Atlantis have been lost, too.

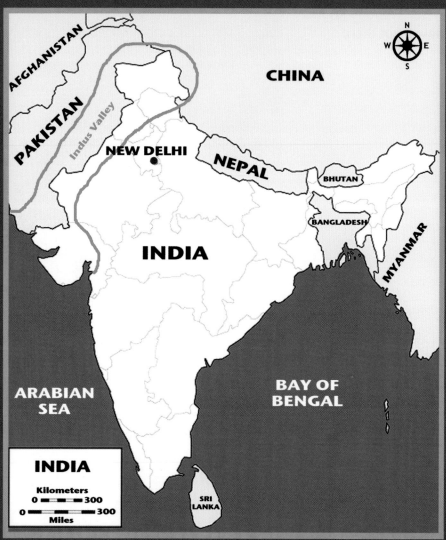

Once a race of people lived in the Indus Valley, outlined in green. They had a very advanced civilization. But they are no longer there. What happened to them? Their fate is a mystery.

Missing People

Where are the people of Atlantis? Did they escape? Drown? You might think it is hard to lose so many people, but it has happened before.

There is a place in India called the Indus Valley. A race of people lived there in 3000 BCE in very advanced and well-planned cities. They lived in brick homes with bathrooms inside. They grew cotton for cloth. They made pottery, and children played with clay toys.

At first this might not sound impressive, but it is. It took people in Europe thousands more years before they lived like that.

It is hard to believe that something bad might have happened in such a peaceful-looking place as the Indus Valley. We can only guess what happened to the people who used to live there. Were they destroyed by war, disease, or a natural disaster?

The Indus Valley people disappeared. Why? No one knows. Did a fire destroy them? Flood? Earthquake? **Invasion** by enemies?

That is a mystery from long ago. A more recent mystery happened in North America.

Just a few hundred years ago, in 1587, about 120 people sailed to Virginia from

England. They lived on Roanoke Island. Three years later, they were all gone. No one knows what happened to them. They were never found.

It is not unusual for people to vanish. These are just two examples, but there are many more. History is filled with them.

Where did the people of Atlantis go? Some believe they went to another country, maybe Egypt or Greece. Others think they fled to South America. Maybe the people of Atlantis built the pyramids in Egypt and the ones in South America. Maybe they built the great cities of Greece. The pyramids and great cities are the mark of an advanced civilization, one like Atlantis. Did people from Atlantis who escaped the destruction go to other parts of Earth and spread their knowledge, such as how to build pyramids?

No one knows. These are all theories. Theories put together what is known to try to answer questions. They suggest strong possibilities. Theories make people think.

The Trojan Horse that the Greeks used to sneak soldiers into Troy with may have looked much like this statue. The trick enabled the Greeks to capture the city and win the war against Troy.

Atlantis Found?

Maybe Atlantis is not lost. Maybe it has already been found.

That idea is not as unusual as it sounds. It has to do with the ancient city of Troy. The people there fought a war with Greece, probably around 1200 BCE. The Greeks used the Trojan Horse to win the battle. They destroyed the city.

Like Atlantis, there were no cameras or newspapers when Troy existed. Over time, many people forgot about it. When the story of Troy was written down about 350 years after its destruction, no one knew if it was true or not. For centuries people did not believe Troy ever existed. They thought it was a **legend**.

For years people did not believe that Troy existed. These ruins are proof that it did. Are these also the ruins of Atlantis?

Then in the 1870s, a man found the ruins of Troy in Turkey. His name was Heinrich Schliemann. His news shocked the world. Now everybody knew Troy was real.

There is a theory that Atlantis is Troy. This is not as amazing as it sounds. A student of Plato's thought Troy and Atlantis were connected. The student was the famous philosopher Aristotle.

Another man who thought that Troy and Atlantis were similar was Strabo. He was a Greek who wrote about history. He lived about 2000 years ago.

Are Troy and Atlantis the same place? Are these men right? Again, no one is certain. It is another theory.

Another place that some people think is Atlantis is Thíra. Its ancient name was Thera, or sometimes Santorini. It is a Greek island in the Aegean Sea.

The Aegean Sea is not big. It is just 400 miles long and about 180 miles wide. Greece is on one side and Turkey is on the other.

The Minoan people lived on Thera. Around 1500 BCE, a **volcano** erupted and destroyed the island. Half of it sank into the sea. Some Minoans escaped to other countries.

Thera traded with Egypt, so it is likely that Egyptians knew about the explosion. Is this the story the Egyptians told Solon? Was Thera really Atlantis? There are Minoan ruins on Thera. They show an advanced culture. Are these the ruins of Atlantis?

The island of Thíra in the Aegean Sea was Thera in ancient times. Many people believe Thíra holds a key to the mystery of Atlantis. They believe that in ancient times, it held a civilization that was destroyed by a natural disaster.

Has Atlantis already been found? Is it Troy? Is it Thera? Or was Atlantis any of the other ancient ruins that have been discovered?

There are many questions about Atlantis. There are no answers. Trying to solve the mystery of Atlantis is like trying to solve a puzzle with missing pieces. Maybe you will solve the mystery. Maybe you will be the person who finds Atlantis—or proves that it never existed.

Atlantis. Is it fact or fiction? The world waits for the answer.

TIMELINE OF THE LEGEND

14,000 BCE   The height of the last ice age. Much of Earth's water is frozen in glaciers, so worldwide sea levels are much lower than they are in modern times.

9000 BCE   Something powerful destroys the huge island, or continent, of Atlantis.

8000 BCE   The ice-age glaciers have mostly melted; sea levels are, some believe, 14,000 feet higher than they had been 6,000 years before. It is enough water to drown islands and flood coastal areas.

1500 BCE   A volcanic eruption destroys Thera and possibly brings an end to the Minoan civilization.

c. 1200 BCE   After ten years of battle, the Greeks use the Trojan Horse to gain entry to Troy. They destroy the city, winning the Trojan War.

950 BCE   Another possible date, instead of 9000, that Plato meant for the destruction of Atlantis. A small translation change of "thousand" to "hundred" would make this date acceptable.

c 580? BCE   Solon, a Greek poet and statesman, learns about Atlantis from the Egyptians.

350 BCE   Plato writes *Timaeus* and *Critias,* describing Atlantis in both.

TIMELINE OF THE LEGEND

c. 350–325? BCE Aristotle suggests that Troy and Atlantis are the same place.

c. 10? BCE Strabo, like Aristotle, proposes that Troy and Atlantis are the same.

1870s CE Heinrich Schliemann discovers the ruins of Troy, proving the city was real and not just a myth.

1882 The publication of *Atlantis: The Antediluvian World* by Ignatius Donnell rekindles interest in the lost island.

1909 K. T. Frost proposes that Atlantis is not in the Atlantic Ocean but in the Mediterranean Sea, perhaps on Crete.

1960 Angelos G. Galanopoulos discovers the ruins of ancient cities on Thíra (Thera).

1968 Bimini Road is discovered by J. Manson Valentine in the Atlantic Ocean, off the coast of Florida.

1995 A diver discovers coral-covered stone ruins under the water off Yonaguni near Japan.

1996 Teams of divers discover five underwater sites of ancient ruins between Yonaguni and Okinawa, from 20 to 100 feet under the surface.

TIMELINE OF THE LEGEND

1997

Aaron Du Val, president of the Miami-based Egyptology Society, announces that a team of underwater explorers has found the ruins of 12,000-year-old temples off the coast of Bimini, sparking hope that Atlantis has been found. There are many objections to his claim, and he never provides proof of his findings.

2003

A team led by well-known prehistorian Jacques Collina-Girard plans a diving trip to just west of the Strait of Gibraltar. The team believes they will find Atlantis on a submerged mud shoal now known as Spartel Island.

2005

Marc-André Gutscher of the University of Brest, France, finds geological evidence to support Collina-Girard's theory. However, he has yet to find evidence of an ancient culture on Spartel Island. He advises Atlantis hunters to keep looking.[*]

*Letter from Marc-André Gutscher to K. Kris Hurst, archaeologist, in response to her article "Has Geology Found the Lost Continent?" posted Fall 2005 at http://archaeology.about.com/od/controversies/a/atlantis05_3.htm.

FIND OUT MORE

Further Reading

Balit, Christina. *Atlantis: The Legend of a Lost City.* New York: Holt, 2000.

Donkin, Andrew. *Atlantis: The Lost City.* New York: Dorling Kindersley, 2000.

Lewis, Ann. *Atlantis.* New York: Rosen Publishing Group, 2002.

Nardo, Don. *Atlantis.* San Diego: Lucent Books, 2004.

Wallace, Holly. *The Mystery of Atlantis.* Oxford, England: Heinemann Library, 1999.

Works Consulted

Abels, Harriette. *Lost City of Atlantis.* Mankato, Minnesota: Crestwood House, 1987.

Bowman, John S. *The Quest for Atlantis.* Garden City, New York: Doubleday, 1971.

McMullen, David. *Atlantis: The Missing Continent.* Contemporary Perspectives. Milwaukee: Raintree Publishers, 1977.

On the Internet

The Mysterious & Unexplained: "Atlantis—Fact, Fiction or Exaggeration?"
www.activemind.com/Mysterious/Topics/Atlantis/
Atlantis—A Journey by the Old Cultures
http://www.atlantia.de/atlantis_english/atlantis.htm
The UnMuseum—"The Lost Continent of Atlantis"
www.unmuseum.org/atlantis.htm

GLOSSARY

continent (KON-tih-nent)—one of the seven main landmasses on Earth: North America, South America, Antarctica, Europe, Asia, Africa, and Australia.

earthquake (URTH-qwake)—the shock that results when pieces of the earth's surface collide or slide apart.

fertile (FUR-tul)—capable of producing a lot of crops for food.

invasion (in-VAY-shun)—the takeover of a place by an enemy.

legend (LEH-jend)—a story that comes down from the past.

mythology (mih-THAH-luh-jee)—the stories and beliefs that deal with the gods and legendary heroes of a group of people.

paradise (PAR-ah-dise)—a place of extreme beauty or happiness.

virtuous (VIR-choo-us)—having moral goodness.

volcano (vahl-KAY-noe)—a high hill or mountain with a hole that allows hot gases and magma to escape to the Earth's surface.

INDEX